W9-BRB-553

Oprisko,Kris   YAF GRAPHIC
Transformers:official   OPR
   movie adaption # 2

	DATE DUE		
1300	3.4.9		
154	3/22/13		
1715	7/11/14		

TRANSFORMERS: MOVIE ADAPTATION ISSUE NUMBER TWO

STORY BY ROBERTO ORCI & ALEX KURTZMAN AND JOHN ROGERS
SCREENPLAY BY ROBERTO ORCI & ALEX KURTZMAN

ADAPTATION BY KRIS OPRISKO
ART BY ALEX MILNE
COLORS BY JOSH PEREZ
COLOR ASSIST BY LISA MOORE
EDITS BY CHRIS RYALL

Licensed by:

Special thanks to Hasbro's Aaron Archer, Elizabeth Griffin, Sheri Lucci, Richard Zambarano, Jared Jones, Michael Provost, Michael Richie, and Michael Verrecchia for their invaluable assistance

VISIT US AT
www.abdopublishing.com

Reinforced library bound edition published in 2008 by Spotlight, a division of the ABDO Publishing Group, 8000 West 78th Street, Edina, Minnesota 55439. Published by agreement with IDW Publishing. www.idwpublishing.com

Library of Congress Cataloging-in-Publication Data

Oprisko, Kris.
Transformers : official movie adaptation / story by Roberto Orci & Alex Kurtzman and John Rogers ; screenplay by Roberto Orci & Alex Kurtzman ; adaptation by Kris Oprisko ; art by Alex Milne ; colors by Josh Perez ; color assist by Lisa Moore ; edits by Chris Ryall. -- Reinforced library bound ed.
p. cm.
ISBN 978-1-59961-481-6 (v. 1) -- ISBN 978-1-59961-482-3 (v. 2) -- ISBN 978-1-59961-483-0 (v. 3) -- ISBN 978-1-59961-484-7 (v. 4)
1. Graphic novels. I. Milne, Alex. II. Ryall, Chris. III. Transformers (Motion picture : 2007) IV. Title.

PN6727.O67T73 2008
741.5'973--dc22

2007033989

All Spotlight books have reinforced library bindings and are manufactured in the United States of America.

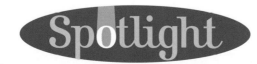

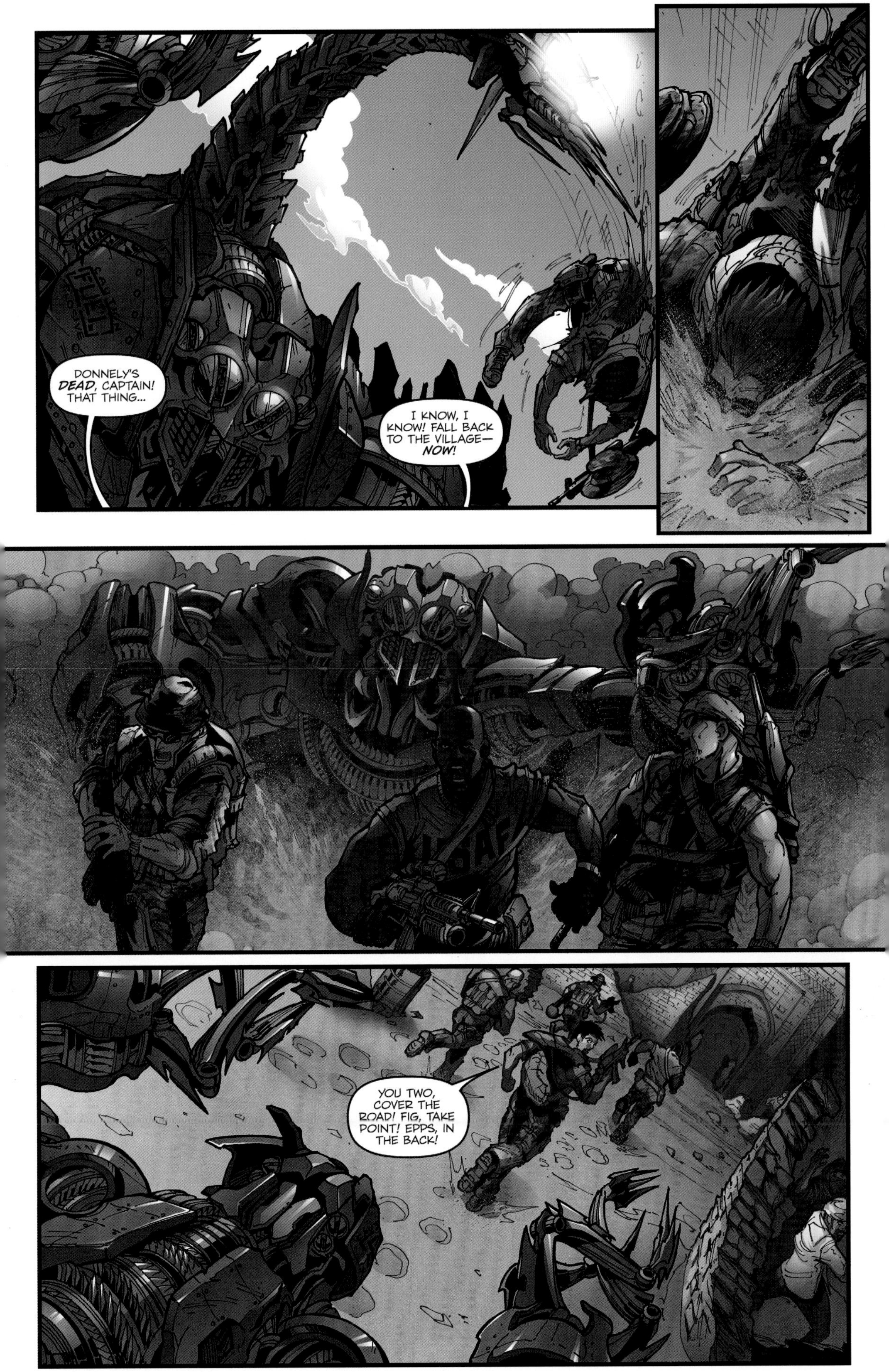
DONNELY'S *DEAD*, CAPTAIN! THAT THING...
I KNOW, I KNOW! FALL BACK TO THE VILLAGE—*NOW*!
YOU TWO, COVER THE ROAD! FIG, TAKE POINT! EPPS, IN THE BACK!

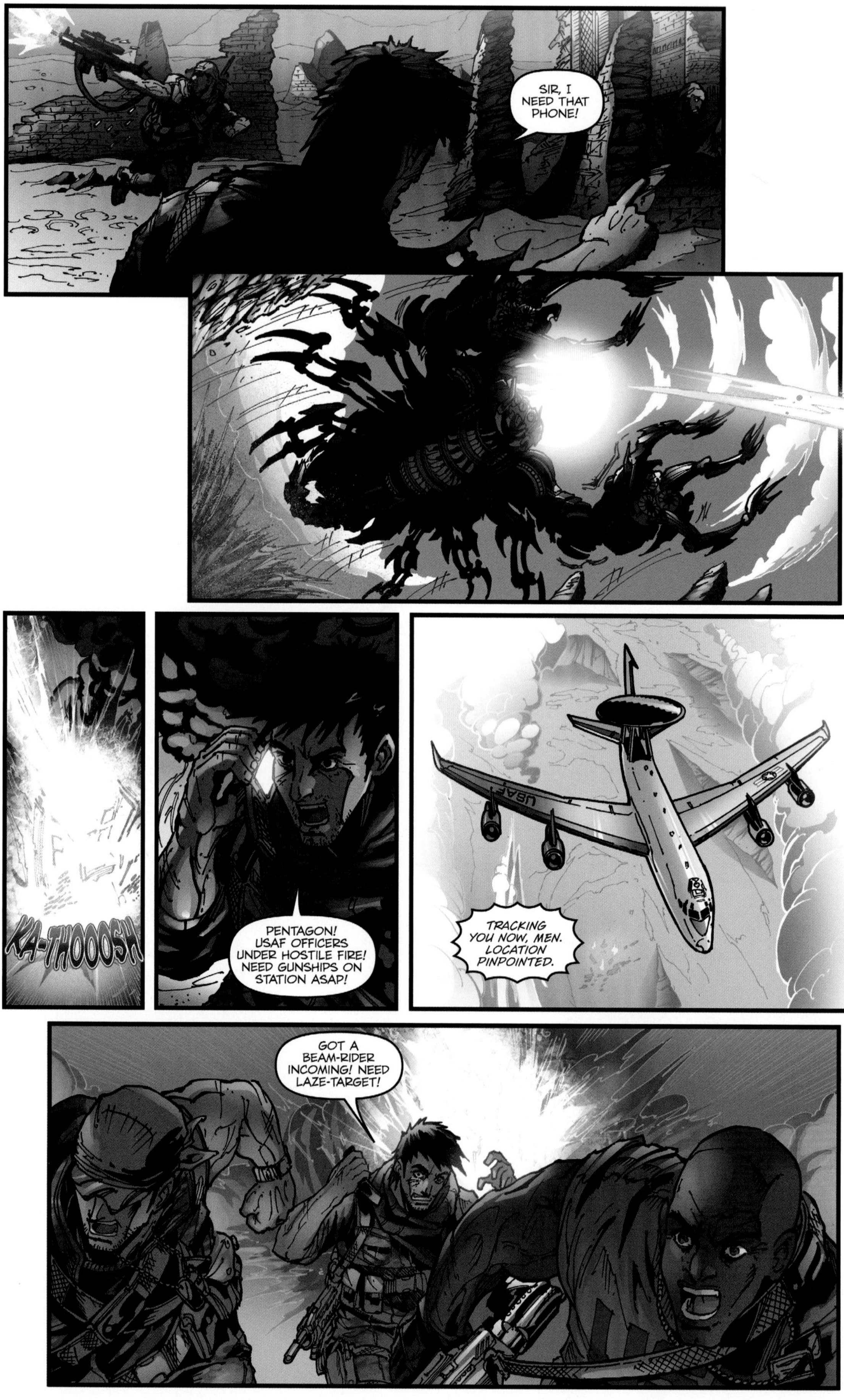
SIR, I NEED THAT PHONE!
KA-THOOOSH
PENTAGON! USAF OFFICERS UNDER HOSTILE FIRE! NEED GUNSHIPS ON STATION ASAP!
USAF
TRACKING YOU NOW, MEN. LOCATION PINPOINTED.
GOT A BEAM-RIDER INCOMING! NEED LAZE-TARGET!

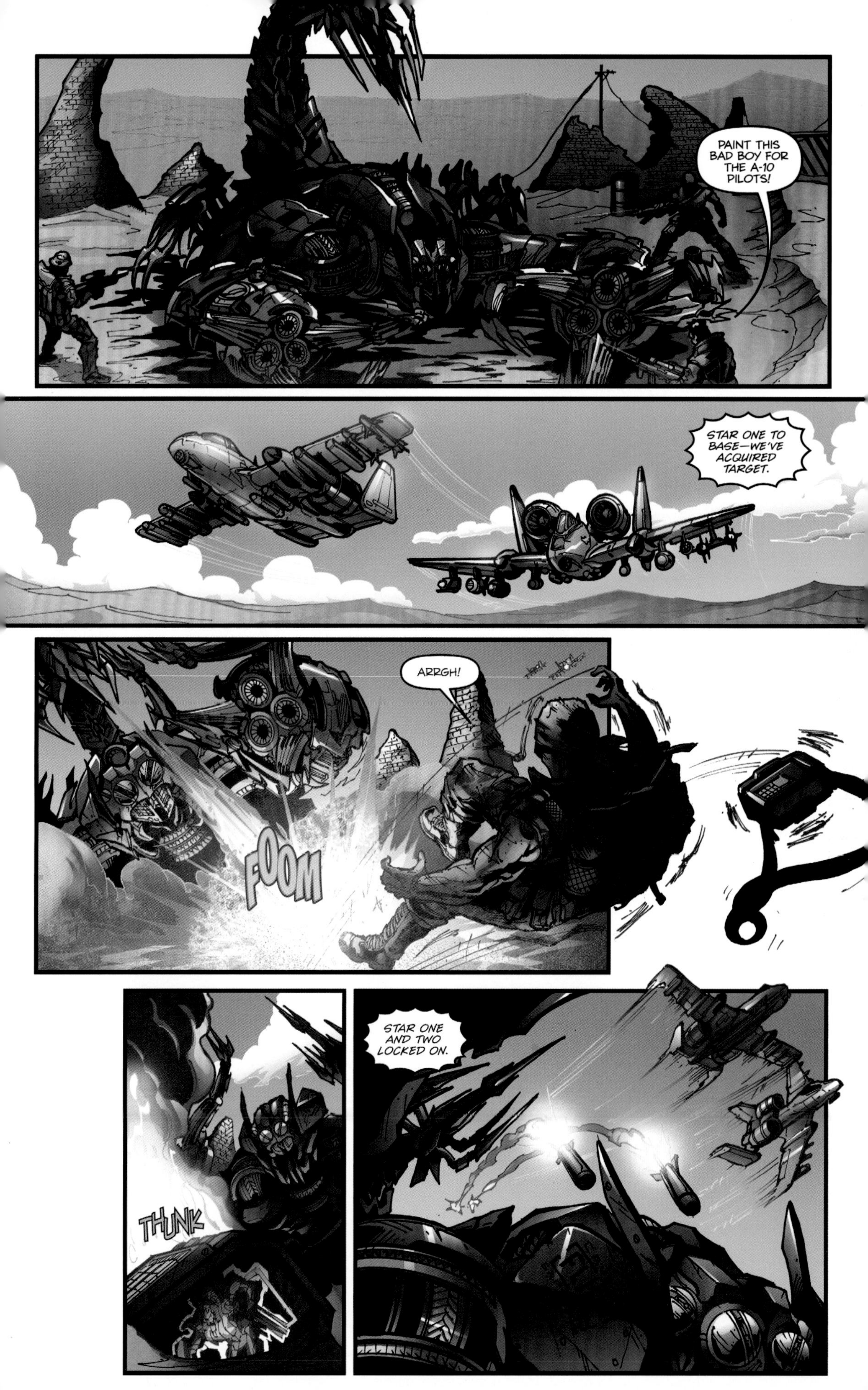
PAINT THIS BAD BOY FOR THE A-10 PILOTS!
STAR ONE TO BASE—WE'VE ACQUIRED TARGET.
ARRGH!
FOOM
THUNK
STAR ONE AND TWO LOCKED ON.

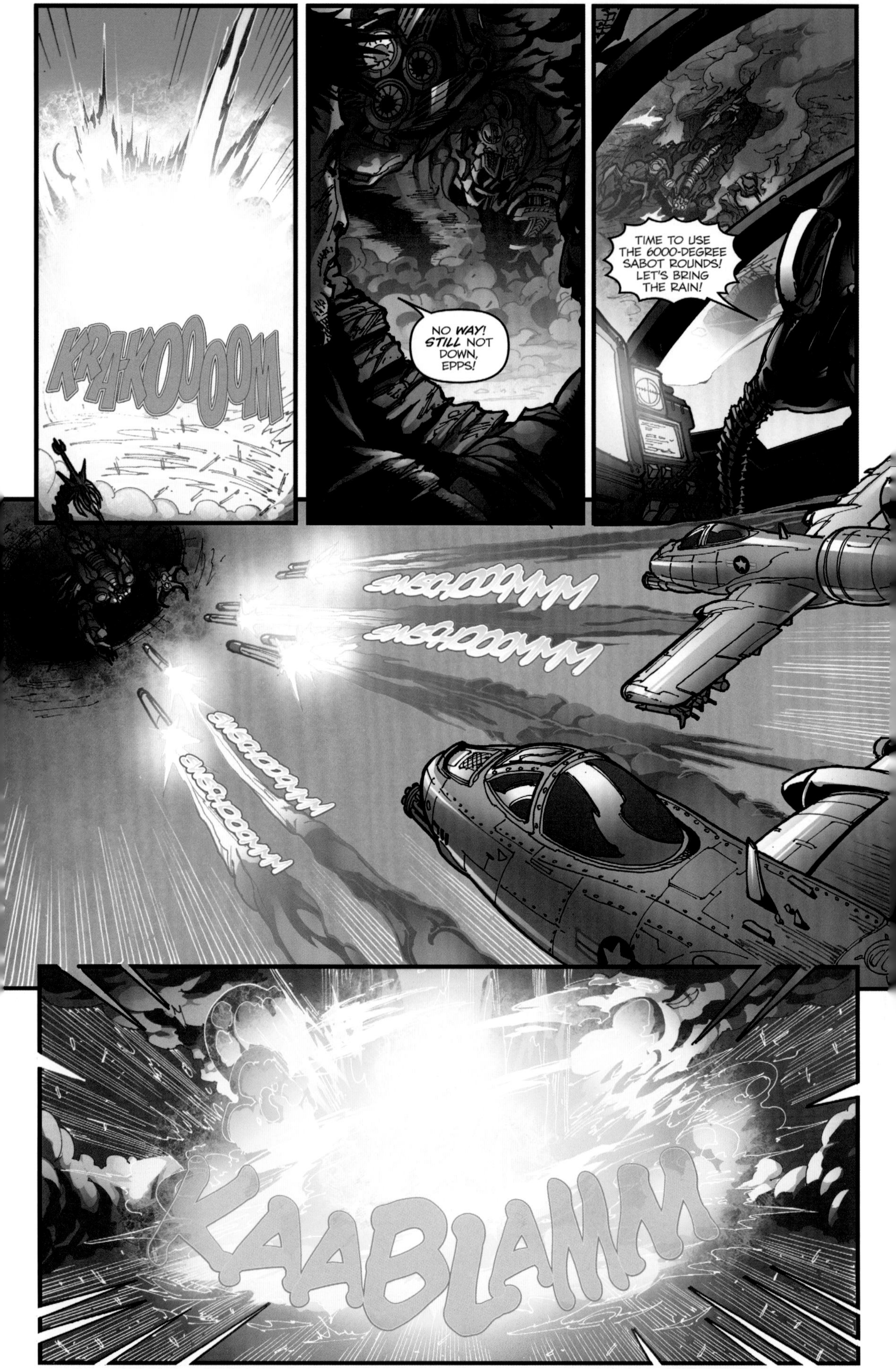
KRAKOOOOM
NO WAY! STILL NOT DOWN, EPPS!
TIME TO USE THE 6000-DEGREE SABOT ROUNDS! LET'S BRING THE RAIN!
KAABLAMM

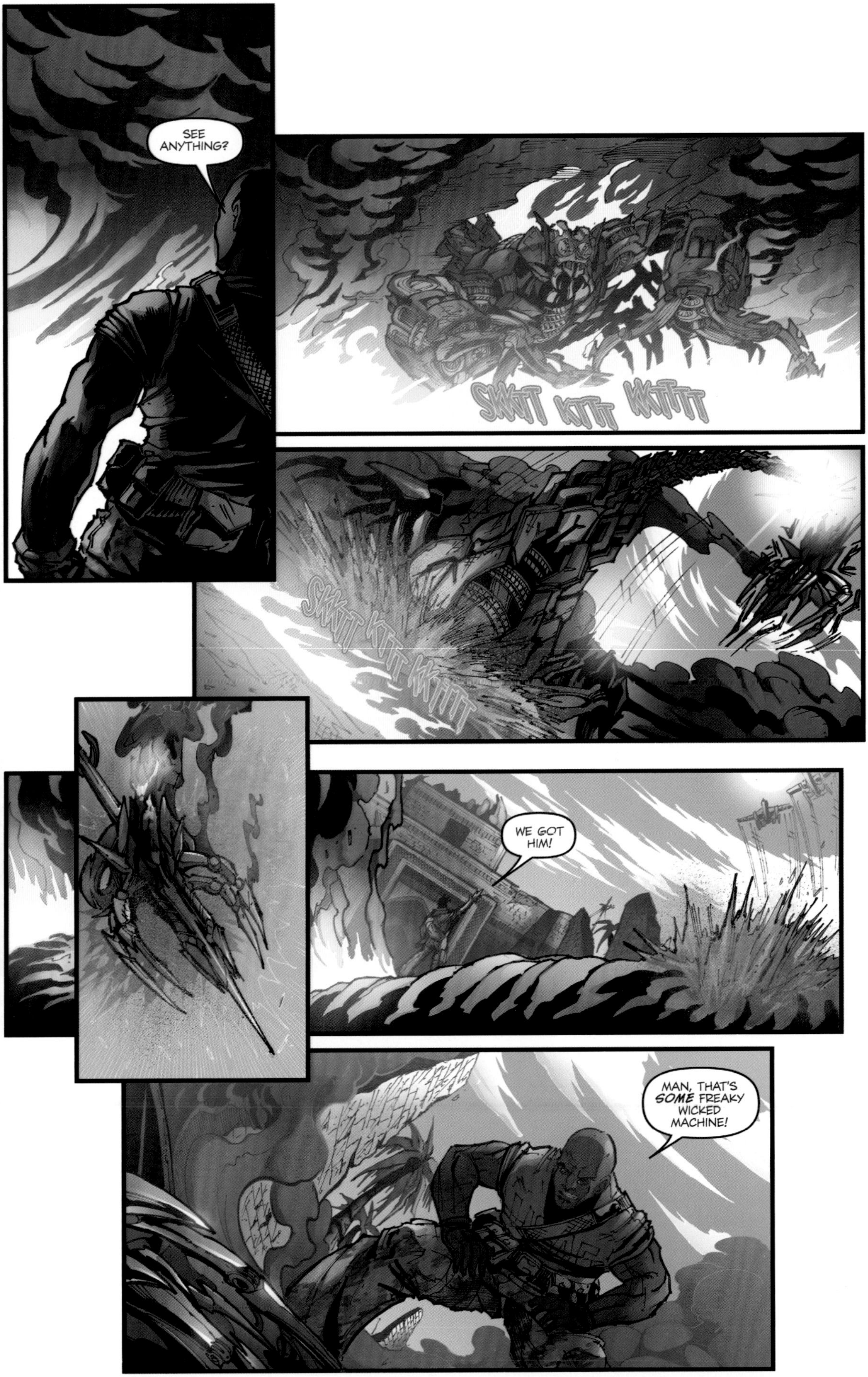
SEE ANYTHING?
SKKTT KTTT KKTTTT
SKKTT KTTT KKTTTT
WE GOT HIM!
MAN, THAT'S *SOME* FREAKY WICKED MACHINE!

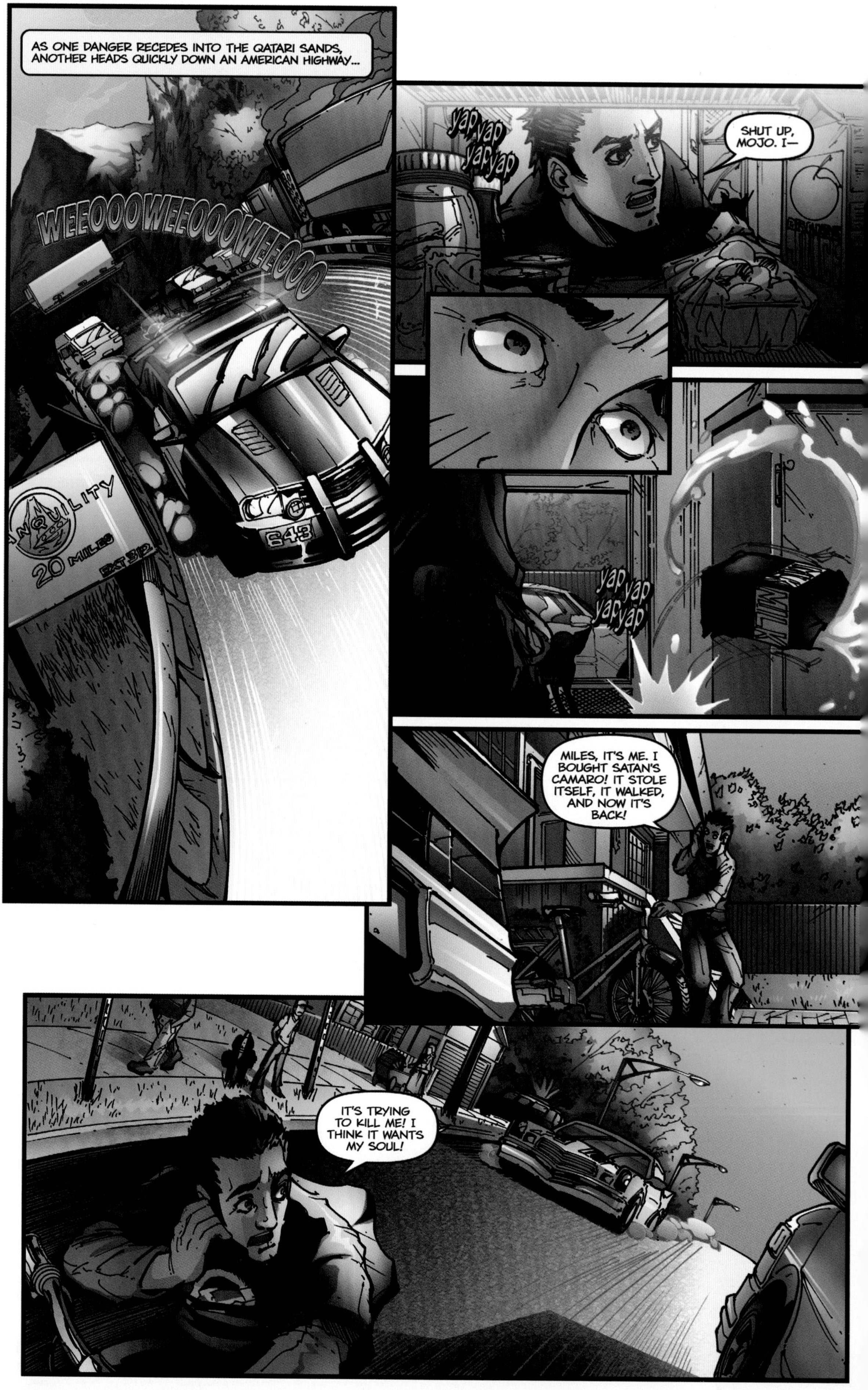

AS ONE DANGER RECEDES INTO THE QATARI SANDS, ANOTHER HEADS QUICKLY DOWN AN AMERICAN HIGHWAY...
WEEOOOWEEOOOWEEOOO
20 MILES
EXIT 312
yapyap yapyap
SHUT UP, MOJO. I—
yapyap yapyap
MILES, IT'S ME. I BOUGHT SATAN'S CAMARO! IT STOLE ITSELF, IT WALKED, AND NOW IT'S BACK!
IT'S TRYING TO KILL ME! I THINK IT WANTS MY SOUL!

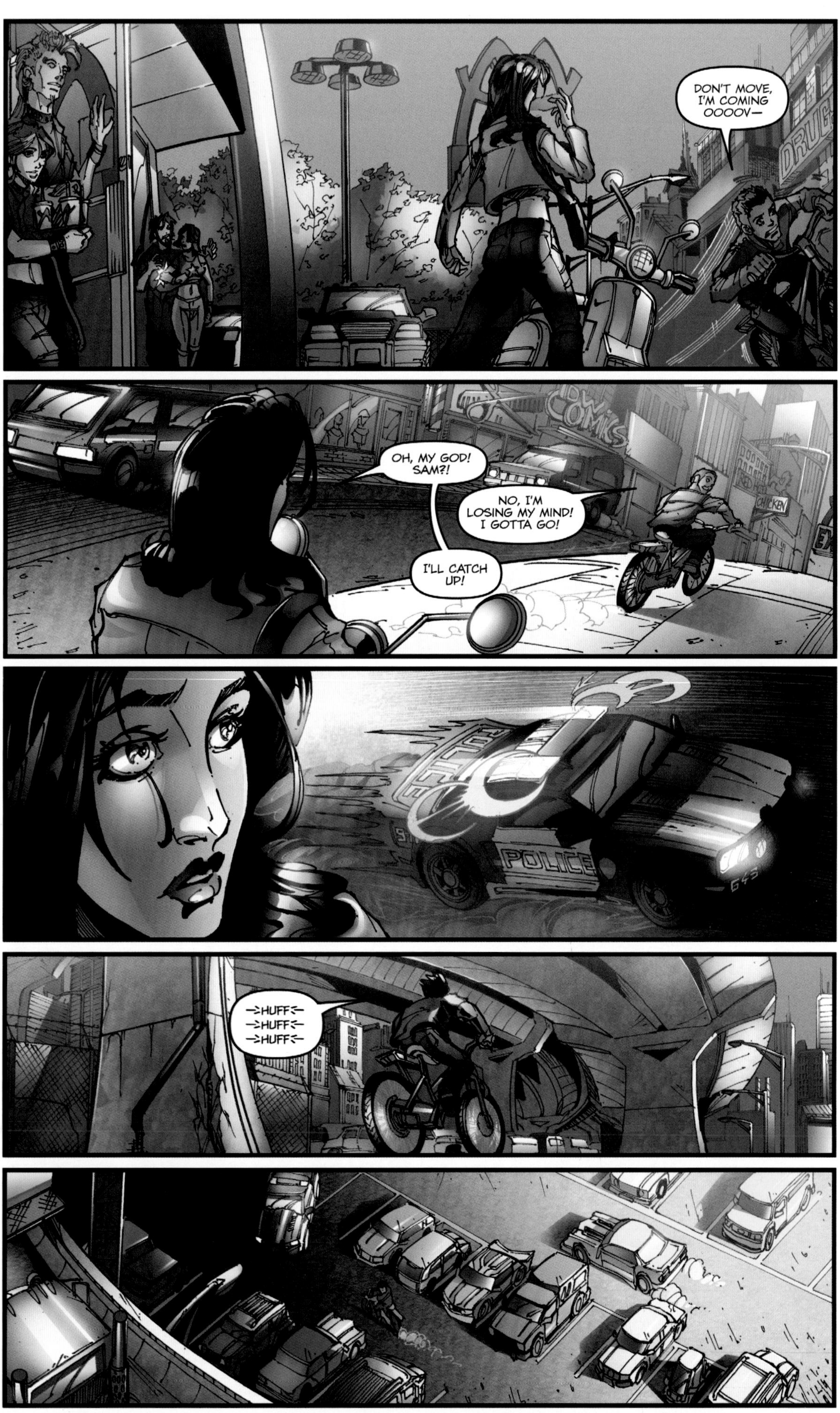
DON'T MOVE, I'M COMING OOOOV—
OH, MY GOD! SAM?!
NO, I'M LOSING MY MIND! I GOTTA GO!
I'LL CATCH UP!
HUFF HUFF HUFF

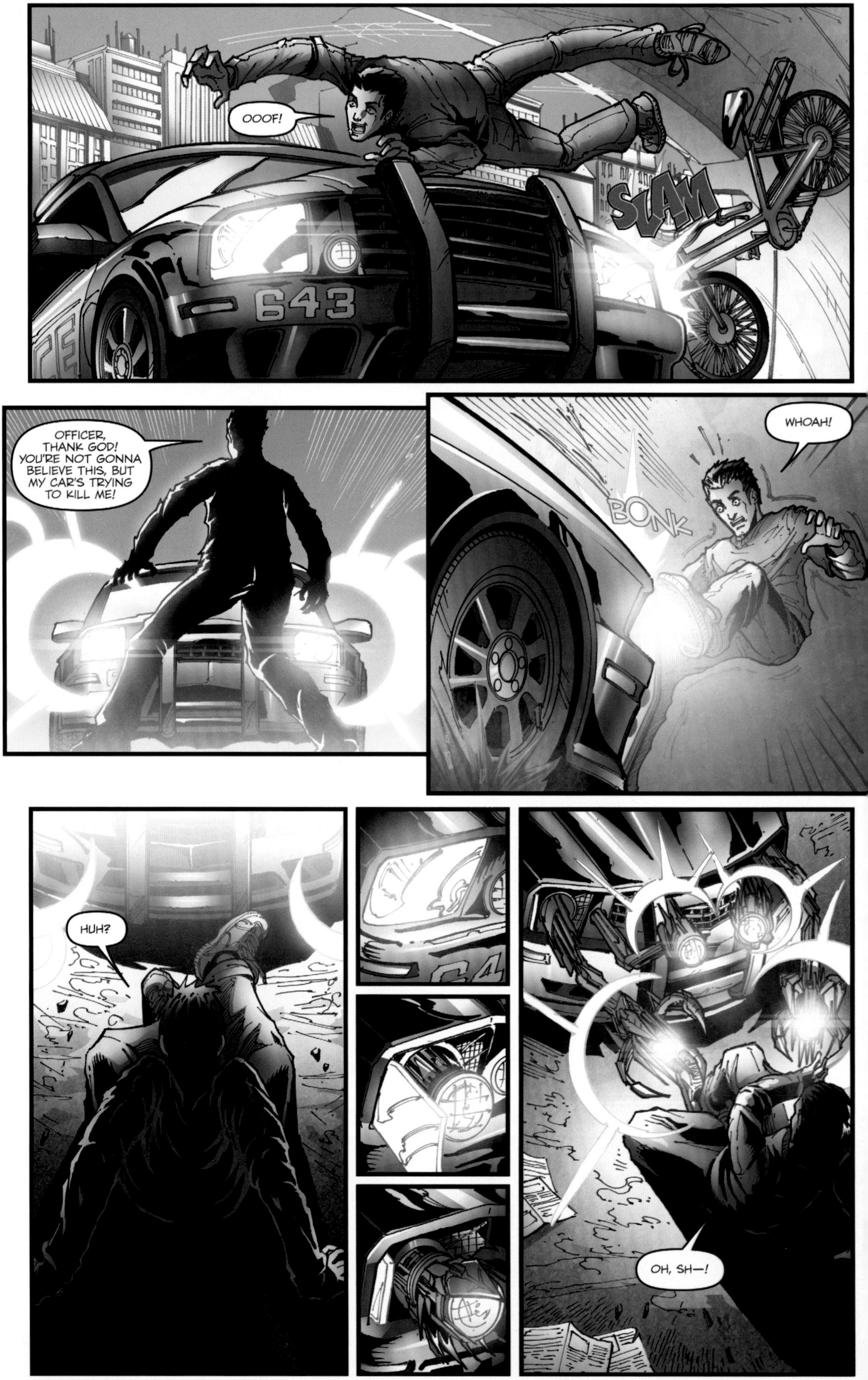
OOOF!
SLAM
643
OFFICER, THANK GOD! YOU'RE NOT GONNA BELIEVE THIS, BUT MY CAR'S TRYING TO KILL ME!
WHOAH!
BONK
HUH?
OH, SH—!

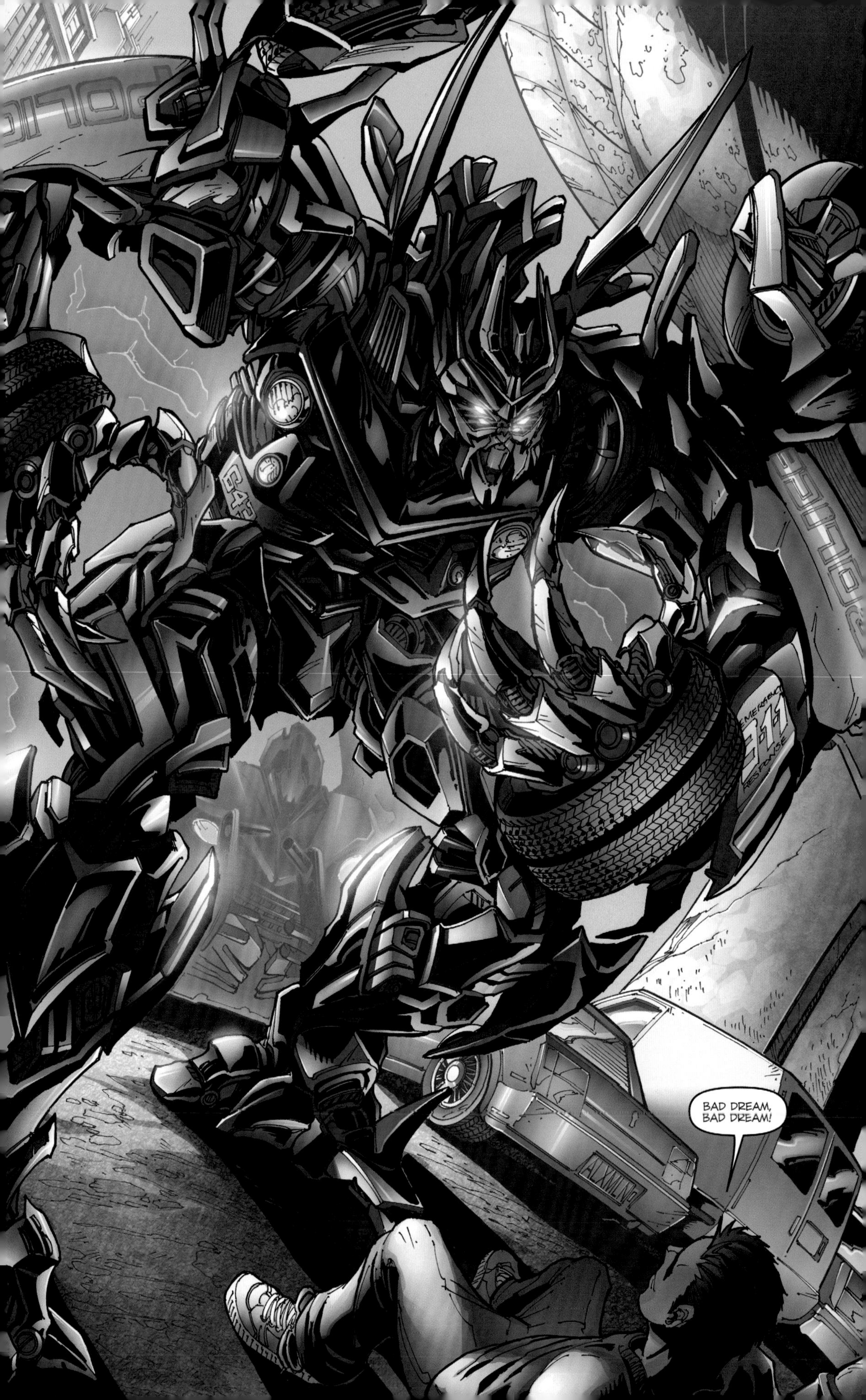
BAD DREAM,
BAD DREAM!

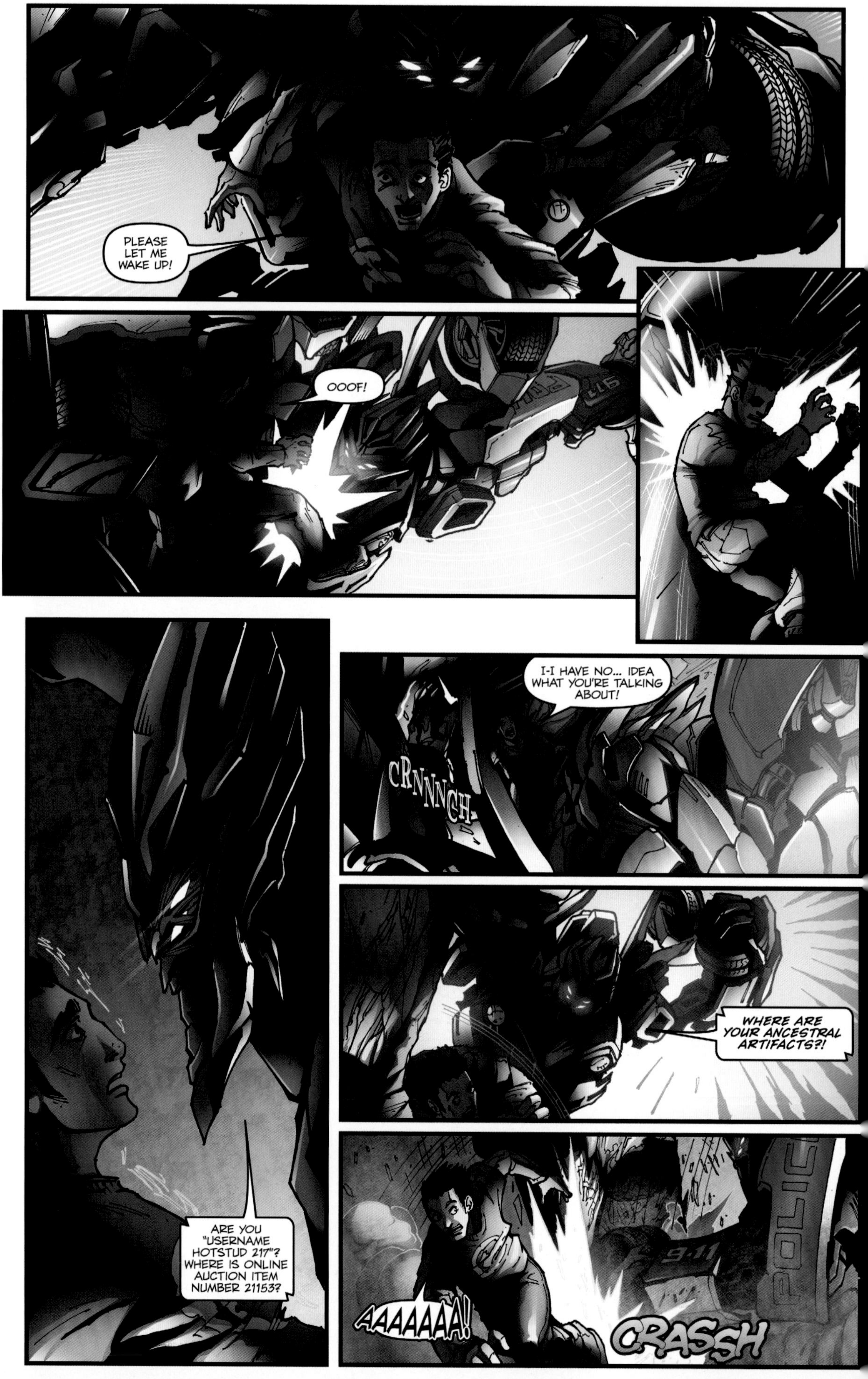
PLEASE LET ME WAKE UP!
OOOF!
ARE YOU "USERNAME HOTSTUD 217"? WHERE IS ONLINE AUCTION ITEM NUMBER 21153?
I-I HAVE NO... IDEA WHAT YOU'RE TALKING ABOUT!
CRNNNCH
WHERE ARE YOUR ANCESTRAL ARTIFACTS?!
AAAAAAA!
CRASSH

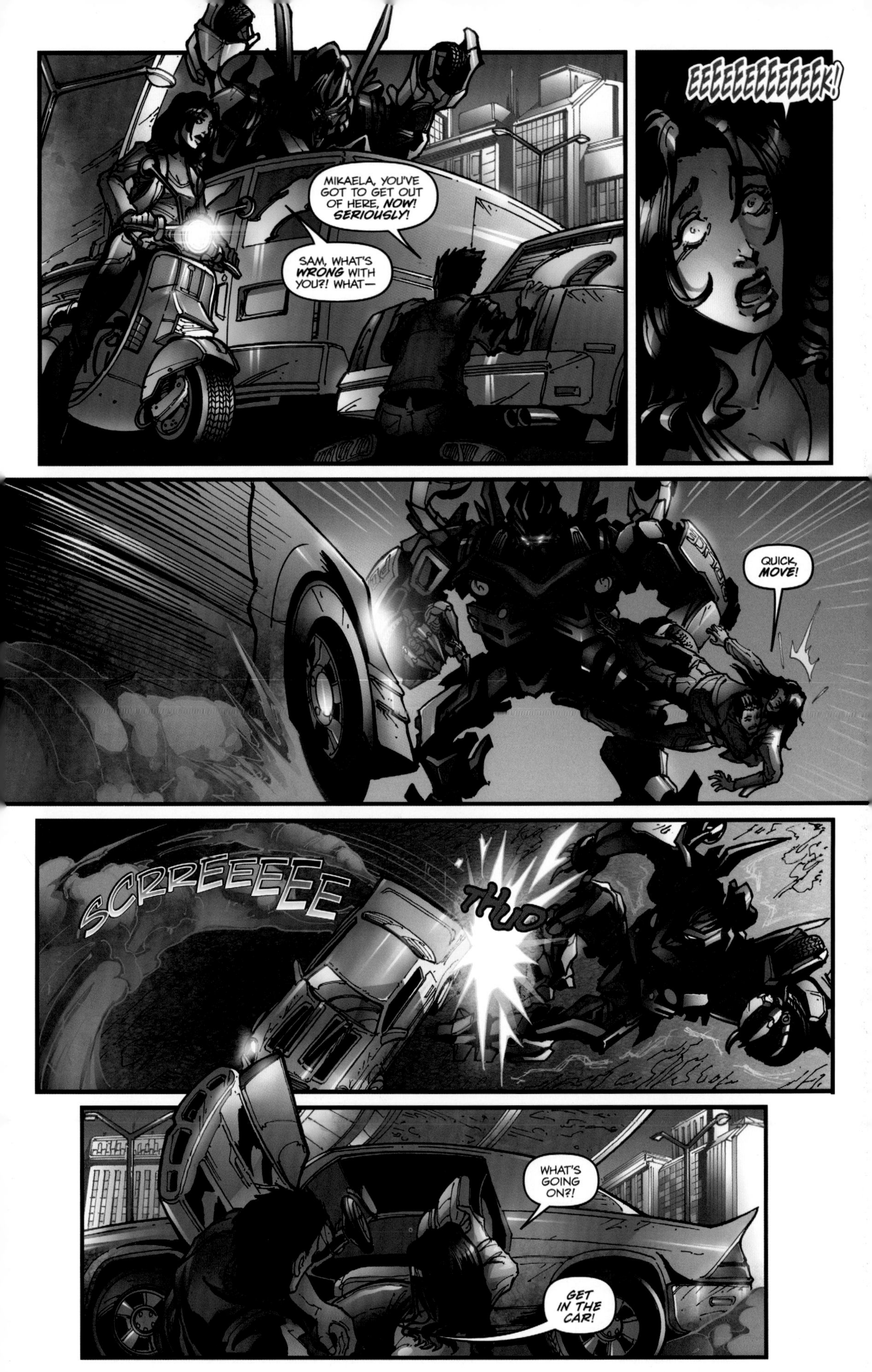
MIKAELA, YOU'VE GOT TO GET OUT OF HERE, NOW! SERIOUSLY!
SAM, WHAT'S WRONG WITH YOU?! WHAT—
EEEEEEEEEEEEK!
QUICK, MOVE!
SCRREEEEEE
THUD
WHAT'S GOING ON?!
GET IN THE CAR!

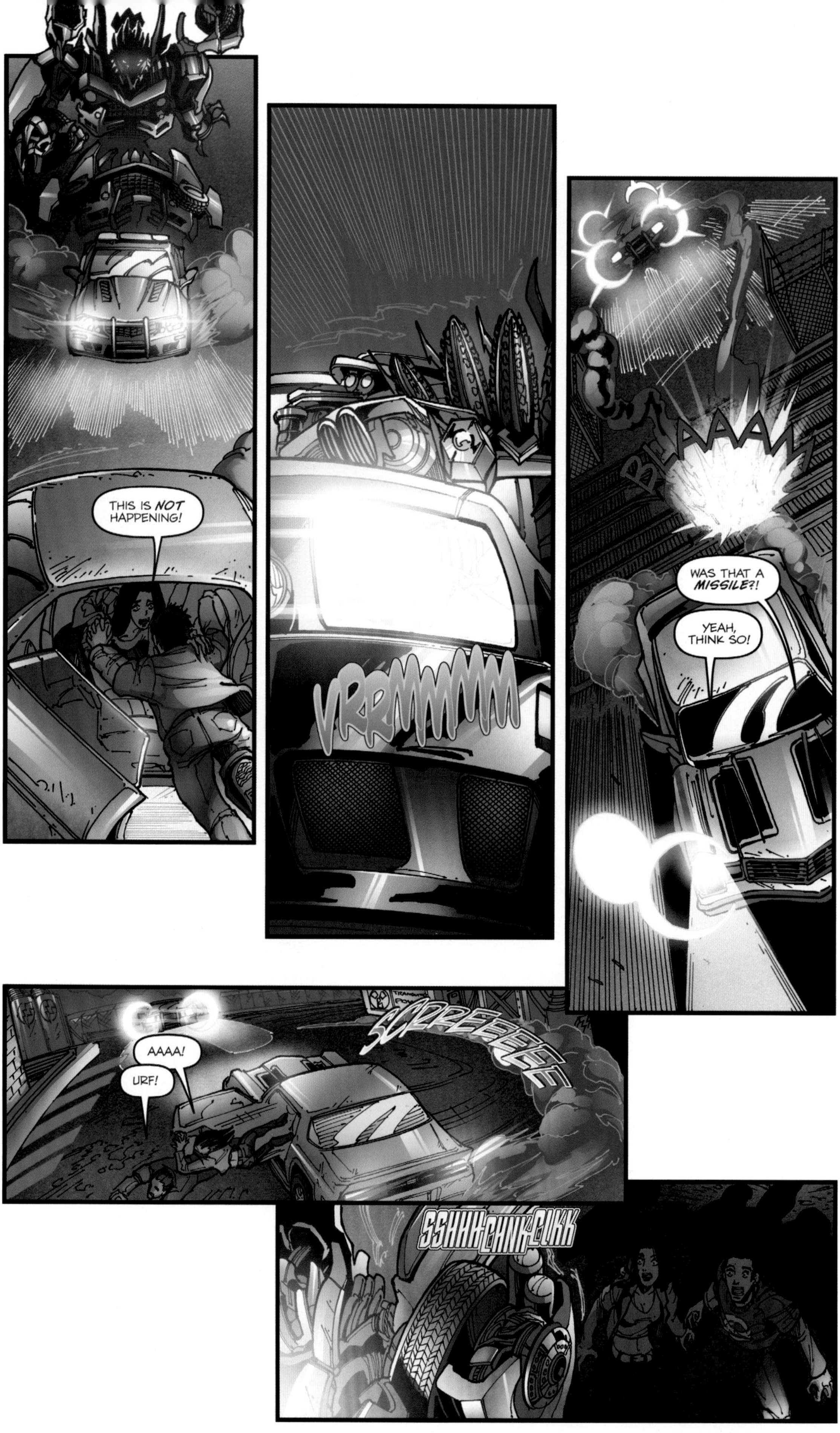
THIS IS NOT HAPPENING!
VRRMMMMM
BLAAAM
WAS THAT A MISSILE?!
YEAH, THINK SO!
SCRREEEEEE
AAAA!
URF!
SSHHHCHNKCLKK

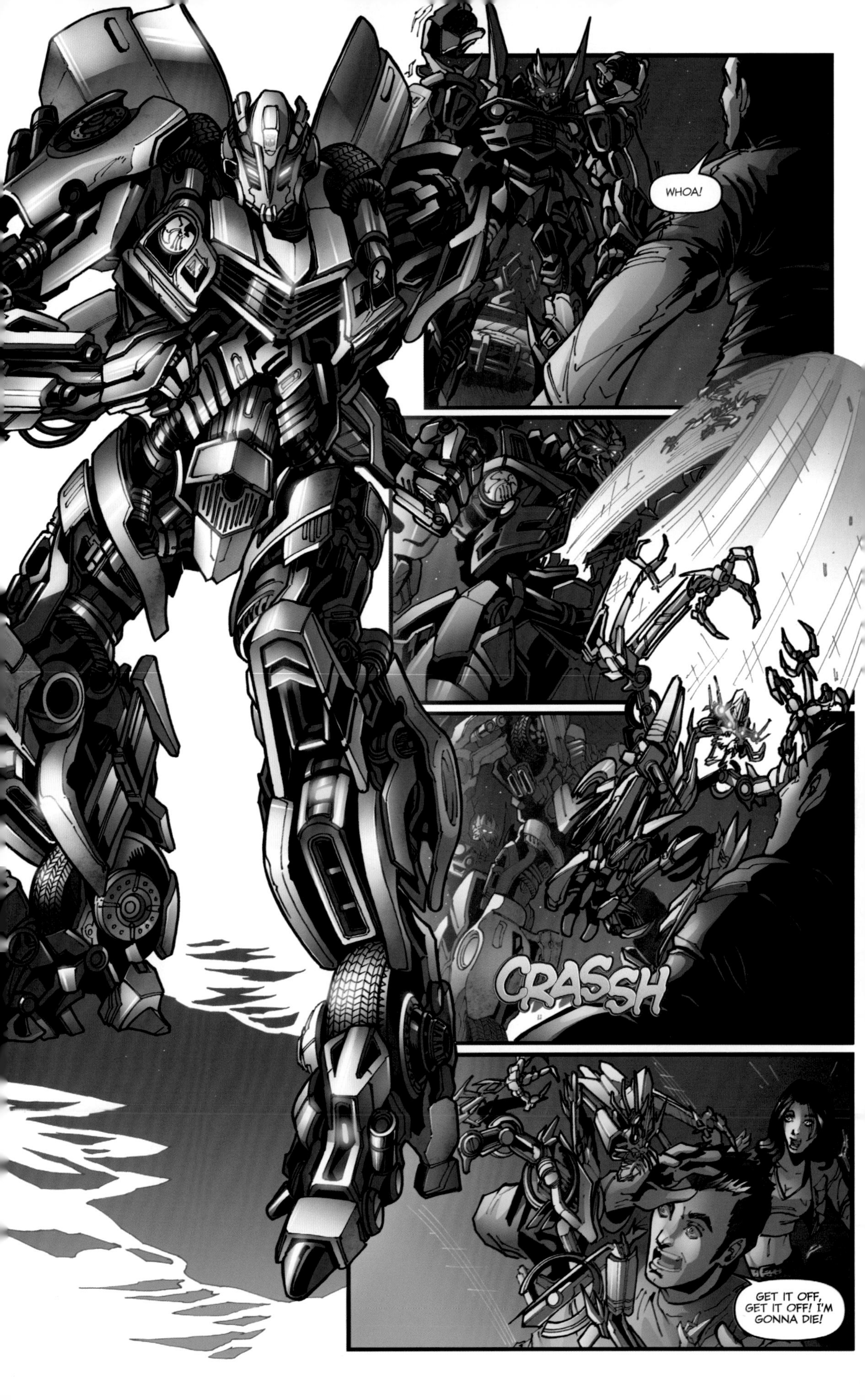
WHOA!
CRASSH
GET IT OFF, GET IT OFF! I'M GONNA DIE!

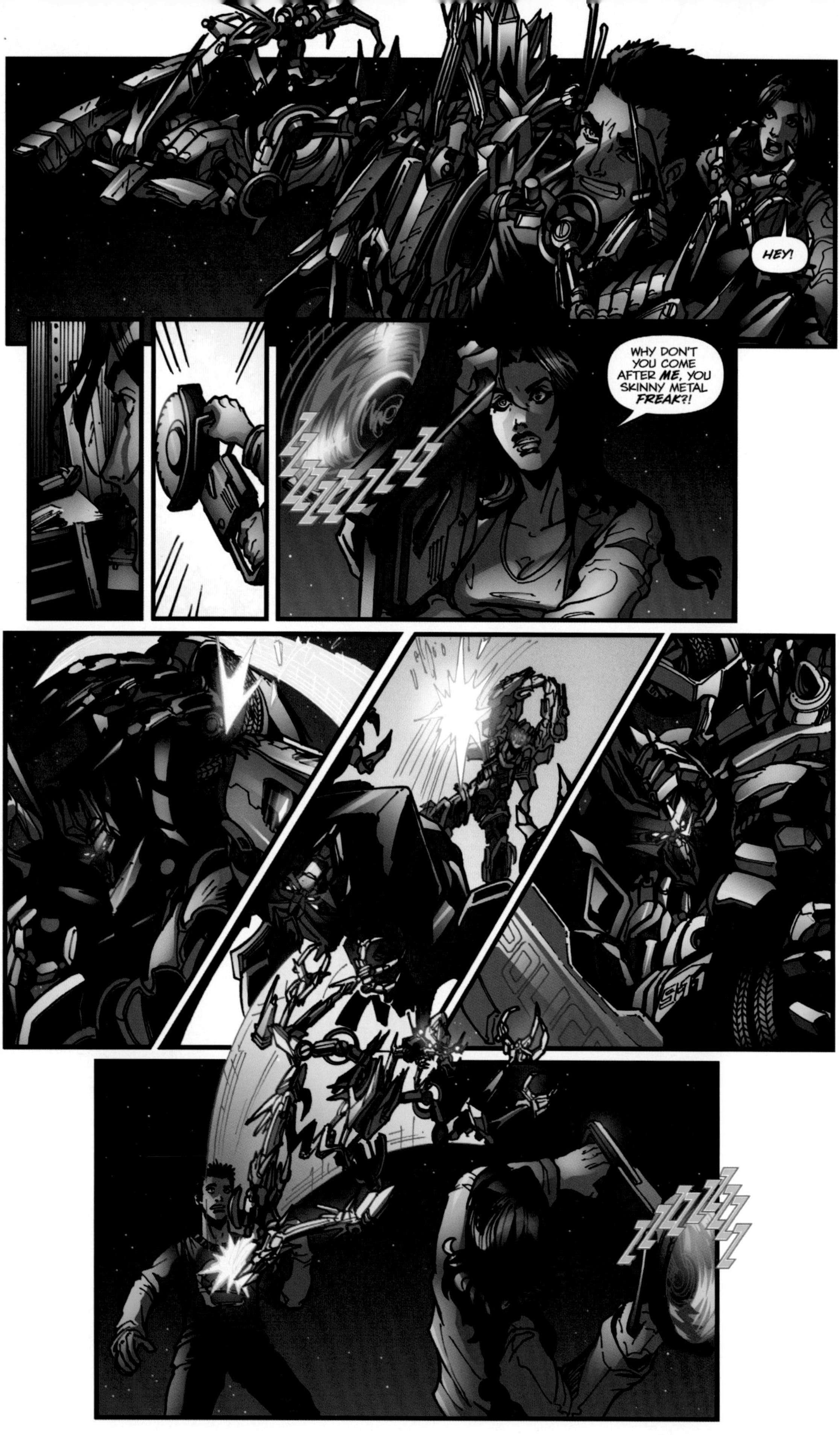
HEY!
WHY DON'T YOU COME AFTER *ME*, YOU SKINNY METAL *FREAK?!*

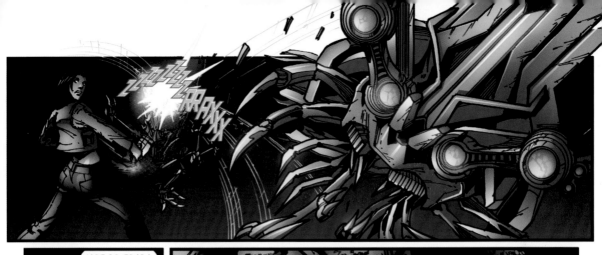

NOT SO TOUGH WITHOUT A BODY, ARE YA?

SAM, LOOK!

BOOOM

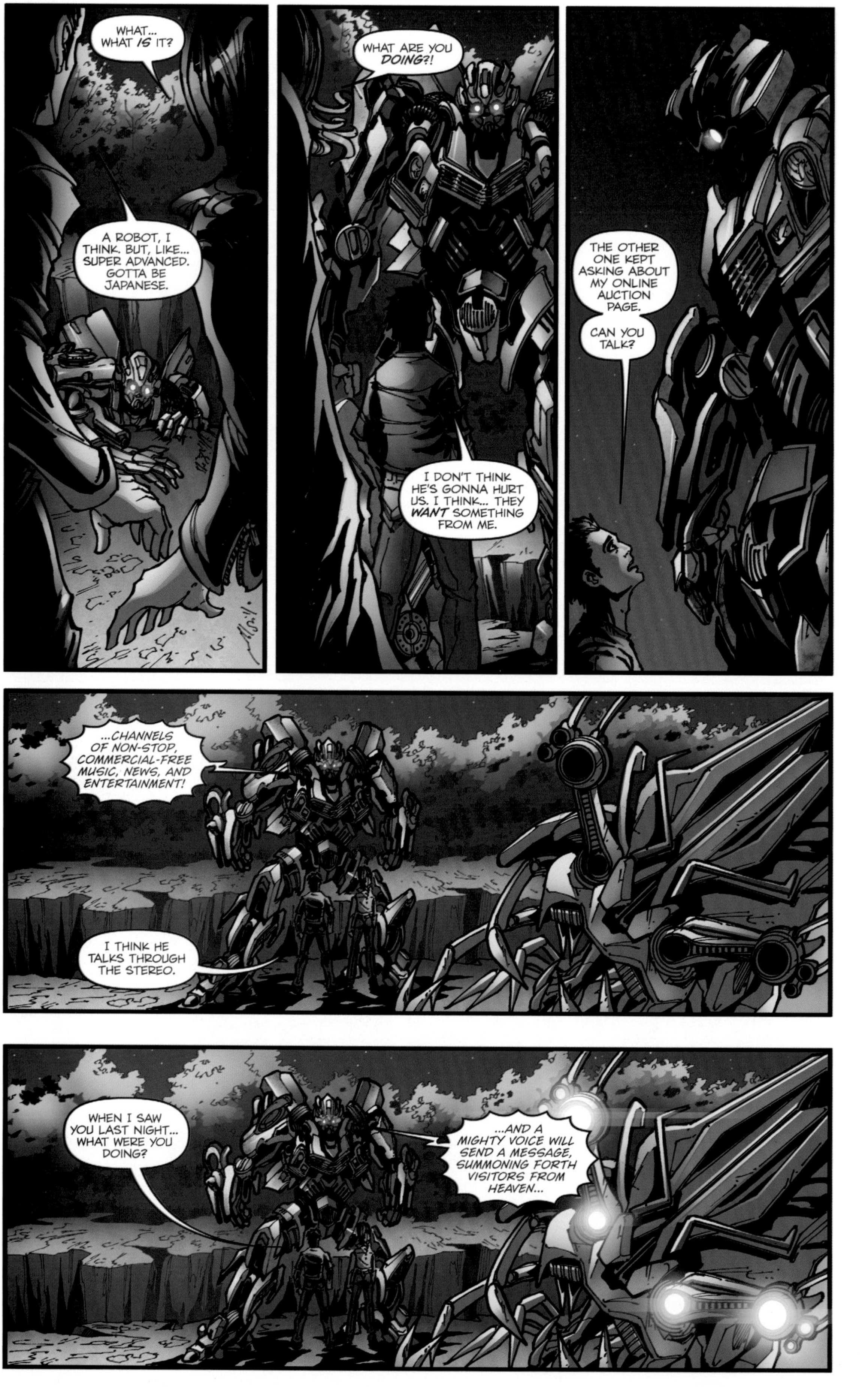
WHAT... WHAT *IS* IT?
A ROBOT, I THINK. BUT, LIKE... SUPER ADVANCED. GOTTA BE JAPANESE.
WHAT ARE YOU *DOING*?!
I DON'T THINK HE'S GONNA HURT US. I THINK... THEY *WANT* SOMETHING FROM ME.
THE OTHER ONE KEPT ASKING ABOUT MY ONLINE AUCTION PAGE.
CAN YOU TALK?
...CHANNELS OF NON-STOP, COMMERCIAL-FREE MUSIC, NEWS, AND ENTERTAINMENT!
I THINK HE TALKS THROUGH THE STEREO.
WHEN I SAW YOU LAST NIGHT... WHAT WERE YOU DOING?
...AND A MIGHTY VOICE WILL SEND A MESSAGE, SUMMONING FORTH VISITORS FROM HEAVEN...

SKRRRICK

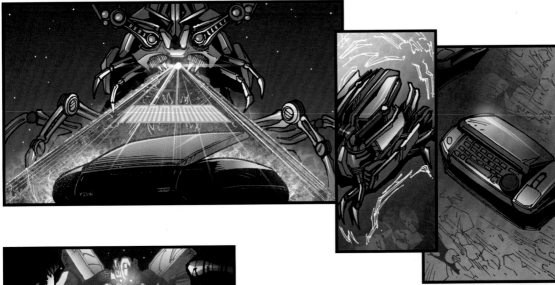

YOU WERE CALLING SOMEONE?

VISITORS FROM HEAVEN? WHAT'RE YOU, LIKE, AN ALIEN?

I THINK... IT WANTS US TO GET IN.

AND GO WHERE?

I DON'T KNOW, BUT THINK ABOUT IT... WHEN WE LOOK BACK ON THIS YEARS FROM NOW, DON'T YOU WANNA BE ABLE TO SAY WE HAD THE *GUTS* TO GET IN THE CAR?

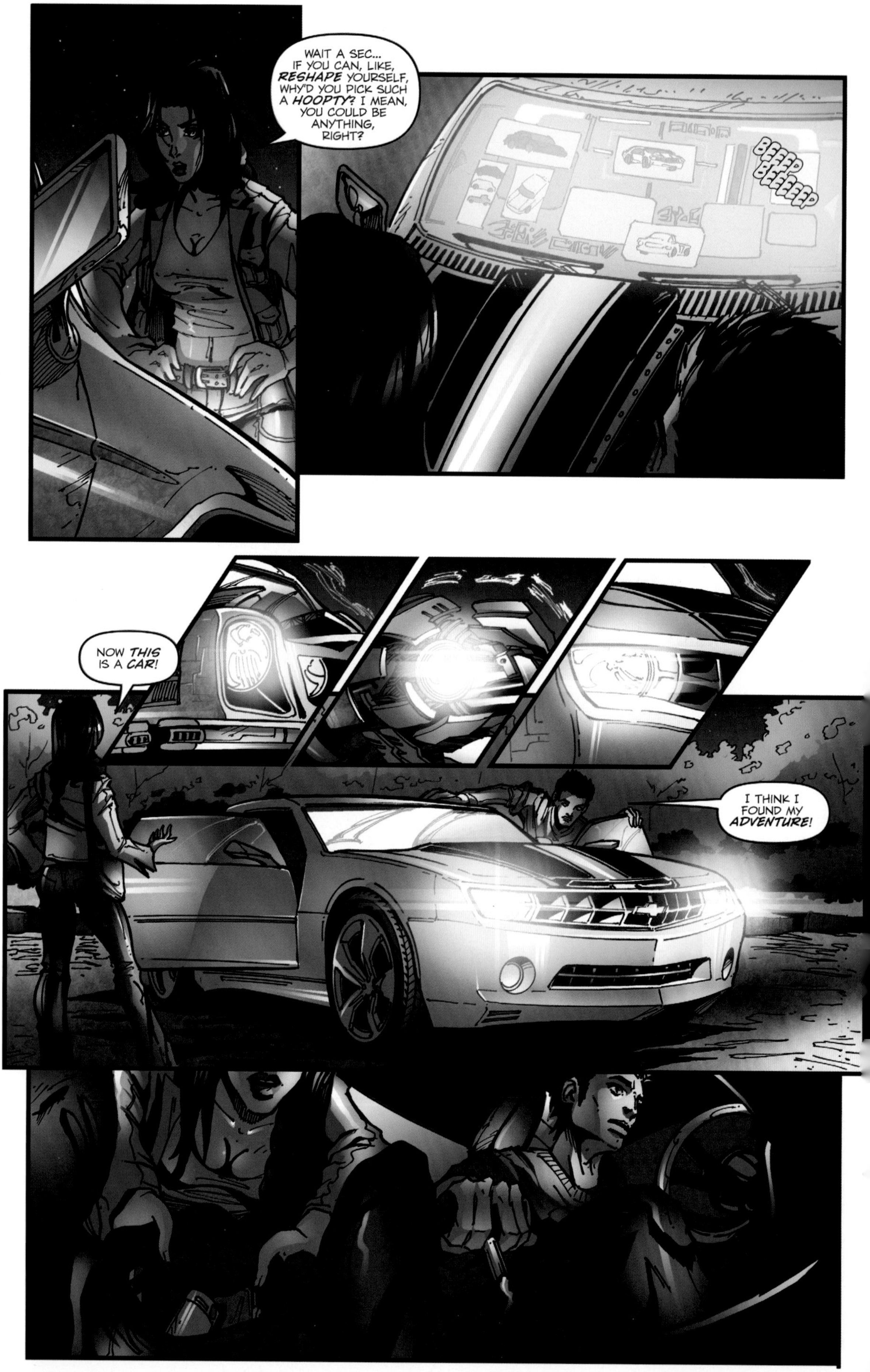
WAIT A SEC... IF YOU CAN, LIKE, RESHAPE YOURSELF, WHY'D YOU PICK SUCH A HOOPTY? I MEAN, YOU COULD BE ANYTHING, RIGHT?
BEEEP BEEEEEP
NOW THIS IS A CAR!
I THINK I FOUND MY ADVENTURE!

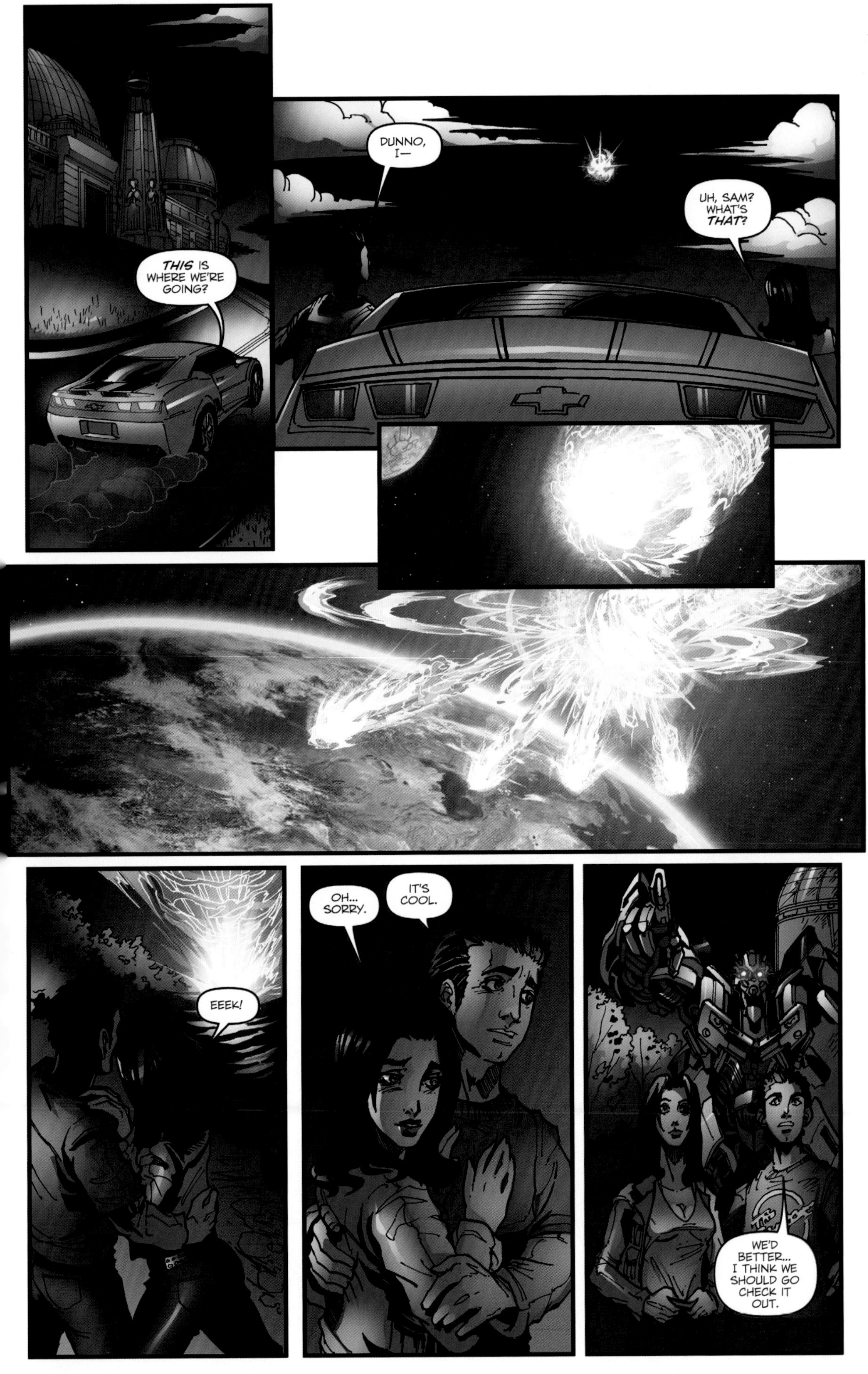
THIS IS WHERE WE'RE GOING?
DUNNO, I—
UH, SAM? WHAT'S THAT?
EEEK!
OH... SORRY.
IT'S COOL.
WE'D BETTER... I THINK WE SHOULD GO CHECK IT OUT.

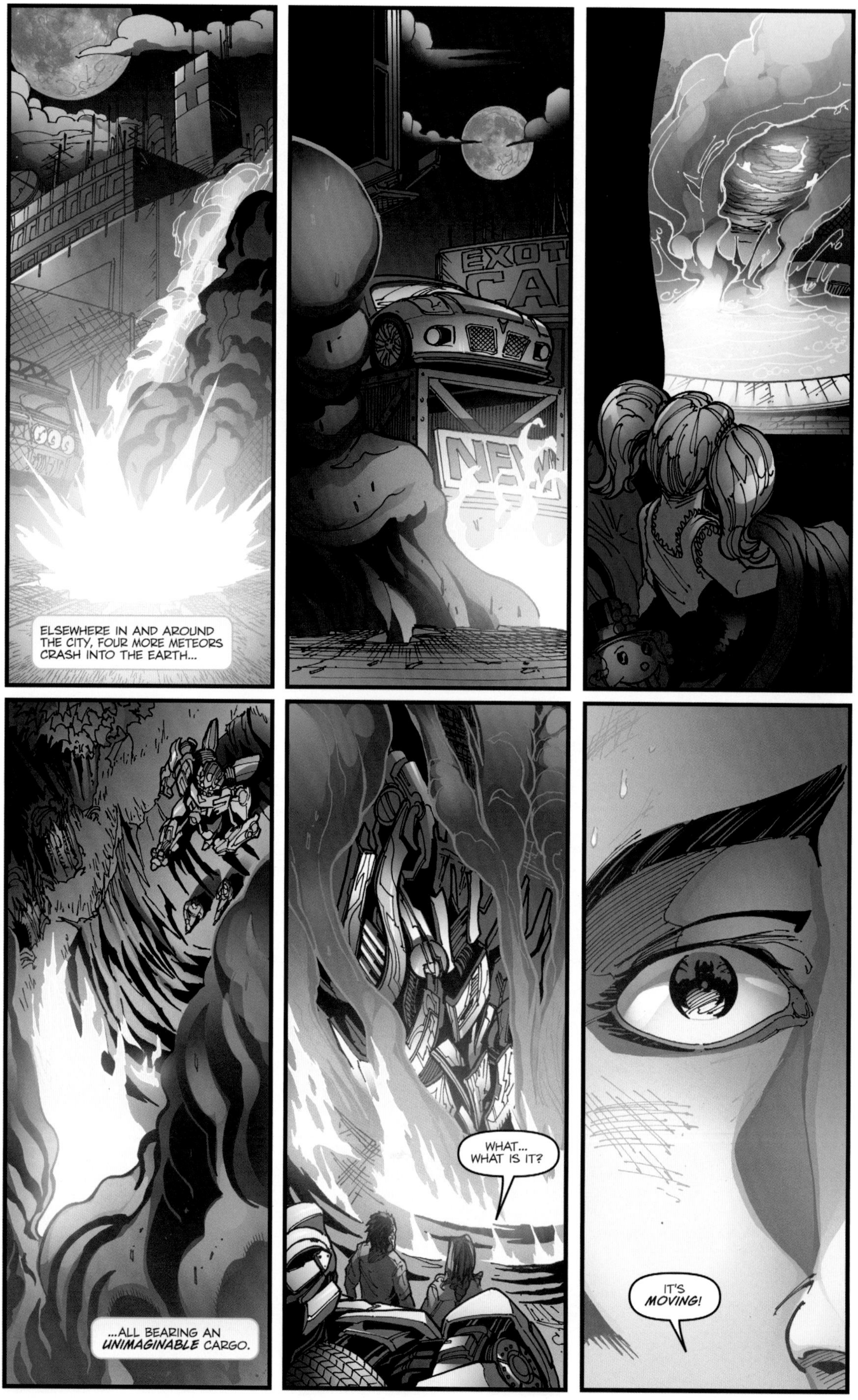
ELSEWHERE IN AND AROUND THE CITY, FOUR MORE METEORS CRASH INTO THE EARTH...
...ALL BEARING AN *UNIMAGINABLE* CARGO.
WHAT... WHAT IS IT?
IT'S *MOVING!*

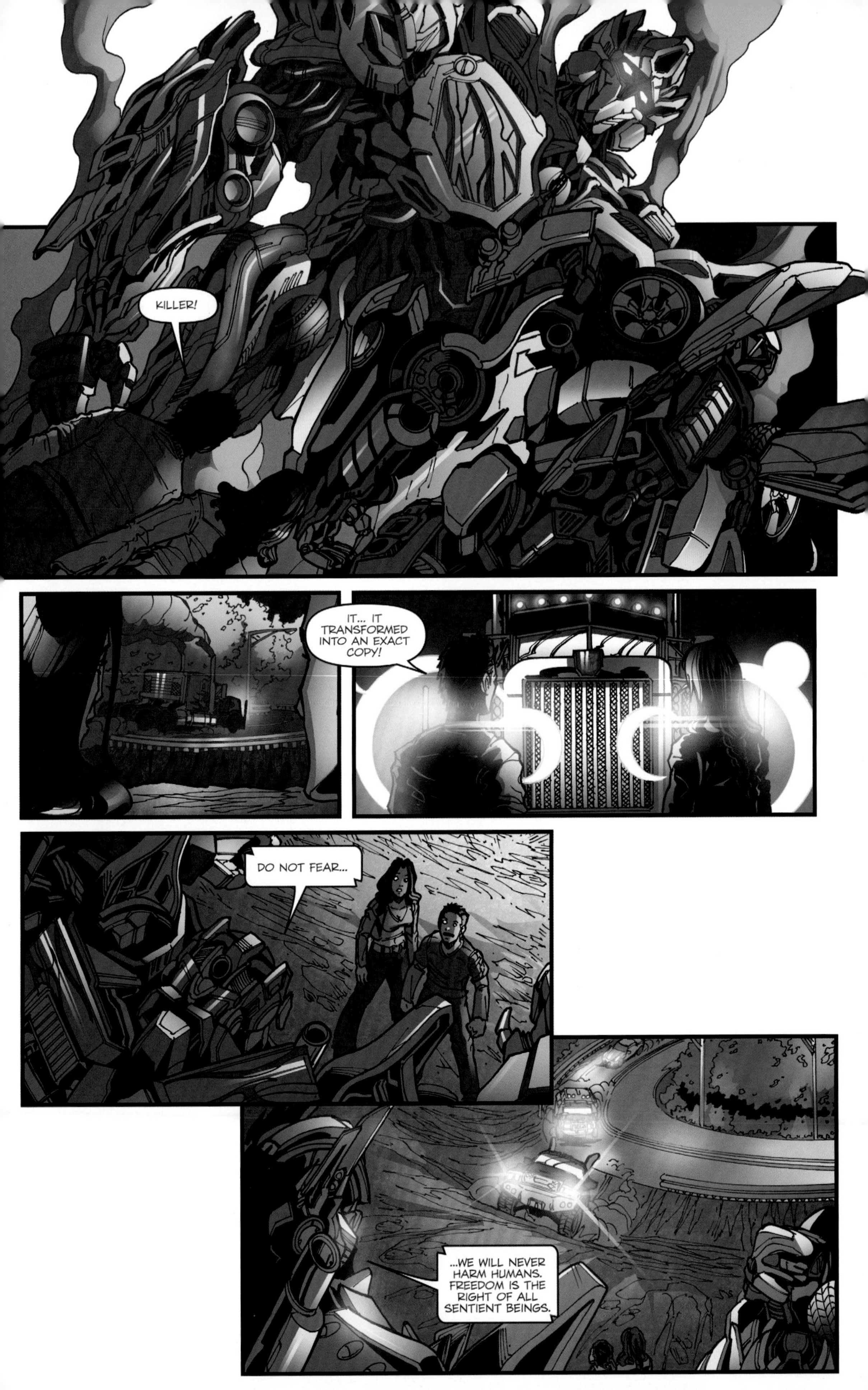
KILLER!
IT... IT TRANSFORMED INTO AN EXACT COPY!
DO NOT FEAR...
...WE WILL NEVER HARM HUMANS. FREEDOM IS THE RIGHT OF ALL SENTIENT BEINGS.

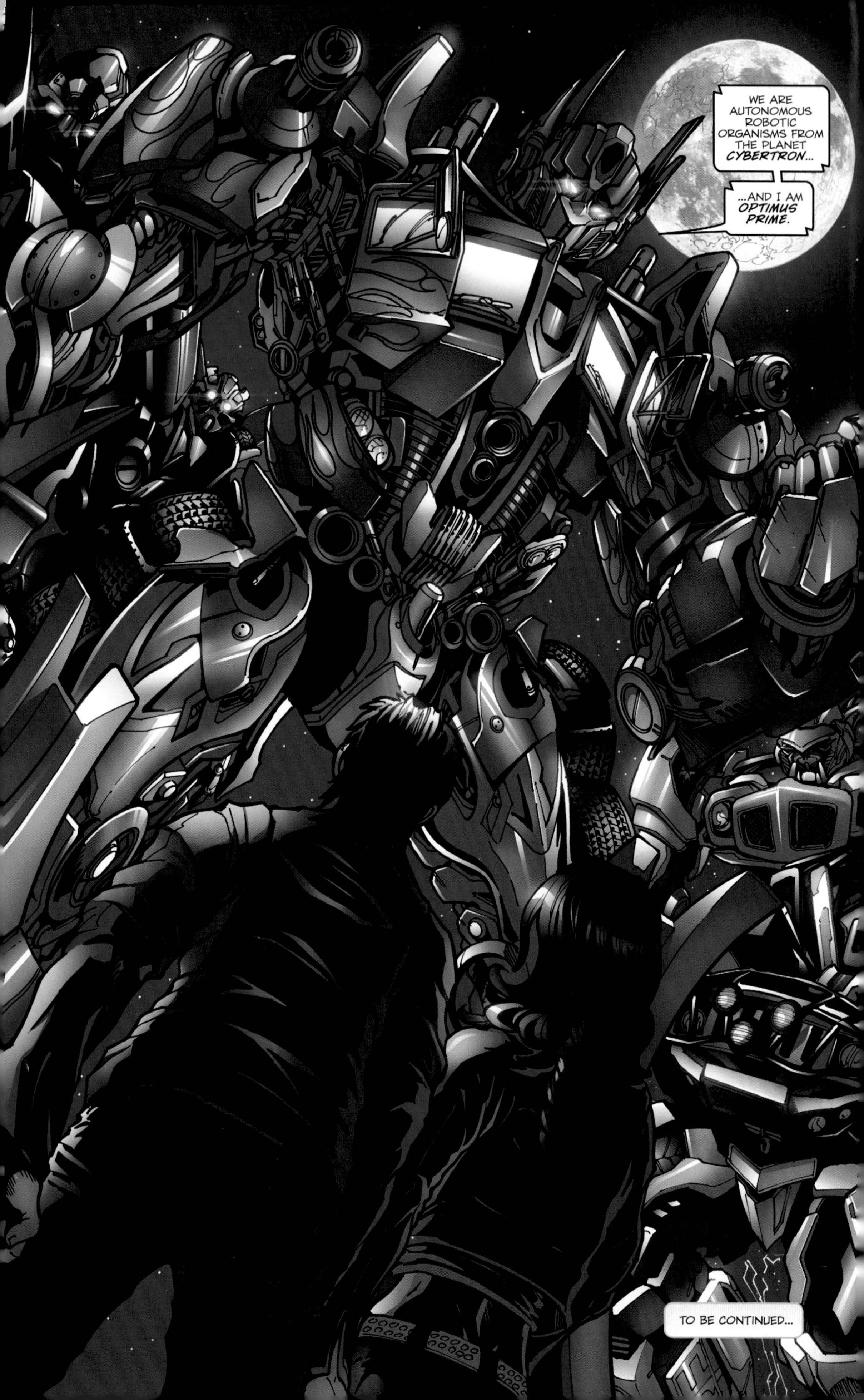
WE ARE AUTONOMOUS ROBOTIC ORGANISMS FROM THE PLANET CYBERTRON...
...AND I AM OPTIMUS PRIME.
TO BE CONTINUED...